WURST DAY EVER

STREET FOOD COZIES, BOOK 10

GRETCHEN ALLEN

SUMMER PRESCOTT BOOKS PUBLISHING

CHAPTER 1

"This is where we're staying tonight?" Billie Halifax asked her host. They walked across the large parking lot that had once held a sea of cars, toward the wall of glass that towered above them. She reached for the handle on the door in front of her, one of about twenty in a row, and pulled it open. The door shut quickly behind them as they stepped inside, shutting out the sound of the real world outside as it closed.

They stood inside the large vestibule for a long moment. Billie had never been there before, but she had been in dozens of places just like it. She looked across the large space to the other side. She could almost hear the din of voices as families and teenagers came and went, in through the glass doors and out through the same. Had it been so long ago that people braved the vast parking lots and hiked long distances just to pull open the glass doors and enter the world inside? She followed her host to the second set of doors and waited while he pulled the door open for her.

Eerie silence greeted them in the large entryway. Billie counted three smaller storefronts on either side of her as they walked toward the large center, the first crossroads of the old, suburban shopping mall. Billie ignored the goosebumps rising on her arms as they walked past the first set of escalators leading down to the level below them. She could hear sounds of life coming from other corners of the mall, but the sounds echoed across the empty expanse almost like disembodied voices calling out to her in a vivid dream.

"This is a strange place for overnight accommodations, isn't it?" Lincoln Mathers, her host, said as he walked ahead of her. Billie nodded but did not vocalize her answer. "Over there was that big jewelry store that was held up at gunpoint back in 1997. Do you recall the stampede that caused? Folks running for their lives right out into the parking lot. The entire mall emptied of customers in a matter of minutes."

"I think I remember seeing something about it on the news," Billie fibbed. "I'm not from the area."

"Oh, I see," he said. They stopped in front of

another small storefront, likely a small boutique at one time. The once open front of the store had been changed to appear more like the front of a small house in the suburbs, but the footprint of the place remained the same.

"What was this place?" she asked.

"Oh, this one was one of my own," he said, pulling out a large set of metal keys. Billie watched as he shoved one of the keys into the double, patio-like door and pulled it open. "This place was once a charm bracelet store. Do you remember those Italian charm bracelets with all of the little links you clicked together? I owned a storefront here and another one in Jacksonville."

Billie managed a smile. "I do remember those! I had a few myself, and they always pinched my arm."

"They did plenty of that, but these stores were always full, mostly of kids. Morning, noon, and night there was never a lack of people coming through and buying up those little charms. And now, look at this place."

Billie did look at the place. The once busy mall store had been transformed into a softly lit oasis. Pale pink curtains hung over the backlit walls casting an ethereal glow over the space. More curtains hung between the sitting area they now stood in and the sleeping area in the back. A king size bed was situated where Billie figured the counter would have been.

"What gave you the idea to turn this space into a room for the night?" she asked. She was sincere in her question. Her host had once been the owner of several small stores in the mall where they stood and a few more across the state of Florida.

"You know, that is a very good question, and one I can answer with a single word," Lincoln said. "Survival. When the malls began to shut down, a lot of people lost their savings overnight. No one could even begin to fathom what to do next, but the owner of this place, you will meet her at the convention tomorrow, had the foresight to use the large building as something else. Debra Millstead is her name."

"Oh, yeah." Billie smiled. "She's the keynote speaker tomorrow, I believe."

Lincoln nodded. His hair was still full despite the age on his face. Billie wondered if the reason he kept it cut longer in the front was evidence of the same hairstyle he had worn back when the mall was in its heyday. "I think you're right. Though I haven't looked too closely at the itinerary," he said. "She would be a good one to listen to on the subject of reinventing a business to keep yourself going. That's what she did here. While other malls across the country were bulldozed to make space for high rise apartments, Debra reimagined it as a convention center and event space. When the whole Airbnb movement took hold, she contacted a bunch of us who still owned our spaces here and convinced us to turn our stores into fancy motel rooms, for lack of a better way to put it."

"I never thought I would rent a room for the night inside a shopping mall," Billie said, shaking her head. "It's also almost like a teenage dream come true."

Lincoln threw his head back and laughed. Long tresses of gray hair fell into his face when he lowered his head again. He ran his hand through his hair and smoothed them back in one movement, probably the same way he had done for the past thirty years, Billie thought. "I guess I never thought of it that way, but I'll take it," he said. "All I know is her suggestions kept me out of bankruptcy court, unlike a lot of my fellow former entrepreneurs. I landed on my feet, more or less."

"I guess it makes sense," Billie said, looking around the large area. "You put a cozy seating area here and there and add a few bedroom sections. It's really like setting up displays inside a store."

"Only this time people really use them," he said.

Billie frowned suddenly. The thought hit her that

she might have to wander through the dark mall at night to find a restroom. "Is there a bathroom?"

Lincoln grinned. "Yes, there is a full bathroom back there where there once was a small office set up. I bet I know what you're thinking, and I don't blame you one bit. No way would I want to traipse all over this place in the middle of the night looking for a bathroom."

Billie laughed. "I guess our teenage dreaming never took practical matters very seriously," she said. "We were just all so hooked on the idea of sleeping in the same place where we loved to hang out."

Lincoln nodded his head. He pulled a small plastic card from his back pocket and handed it over to her. "This works just like a room key at any hotel," he explained. "You want to slide it through the reader to unlock it. You can leave it on the counter inside here when you go to leave in a few days." He pointed to a small kitchenette Billie had not seen before.

"Okay, Mr. Mathers," she said as she took the card from him. "Thank you so much for renting this to me for the duration of the convention. Will you be attending any of the workshops?"

Lincoln smiled and shrugged. "I'm not sure yet," he said. "I've been to several of these events over the past few years. I usually just check my guests in and let that be that, but this one does seem interesting to me. Maybe I will venture over to the old movie theater where everything is set up and listen in here and there."

"Sounds like a good idea," Billie said. "But try to stay away from the one marked with the number six around eleven tomorrow morning."

"Is that when you're scheduled to present?" he asked.

Billie nodded. "Yes, it is," she said. "I'm supposed to present a workshop on managing a multi-truck street food business."

"Sounds like a real snoozer," he joked. "But, if you think about it, it's a very appropriate subject for a convention all about solo entrepreneurship and rethinking the business world as we know it."

"That's pretty much the name of the entire convention," Billie said. "'Thriving in an Ever Changing Business Landscape.'"

"She could have just called it Business Survival 101," Lincoln said. "That's really what this is all about." He nodded cordially to her and walked toward the entrance. "If you need anything over the next few days, you have my number. I hope you enjoy your stay here."

"Thank you, Mr. Mathers," Billie said. She

pushed her overnight bag against the wall and looked around. "I certainly won't be lacking for space."

"Please call me Lincoln," he said with a charming smile. "And thank you for booking the room with me." With that, he opened the door and walked out. Billie picked up the handle of her suitcase and wheeled it over to the bedroom space. She sat down on the ruffled pink duvet and surveyed the room. She wasn't a particular fan of pink, and the space had it in spades. Billie wondered if there was a Mrs. Mathers who might have influenced her husband's decorating choices. Or maybe there had not been one to tame them. Either way, it sure was a lot of pink.

Her phone rang just then. "Good to know I have a decent cell signal in here," she said and pulled it out of her bag.

"How are things there?" Asher Scanlan asked her when she answered. Asher, her business partner and love interest, remained behind on Sea Glass Island when she traveled over the bridge to the mainland for the convention. It was his urging that encouraged Billie to attend and speak at the convention in the first place. Most of the time, conventions and fairs took place on the large festival grounds they owned together. Her food truck fleet surrounded the large metal building set in the middle of the several hundred-acre grounds. The building housed a large commissary kitchen, a space her many food truck managers utilized almost daily.

"I just got into my room," Billie said.

"How is it, staying in the middle of a shopping mall?" Asher asked.

"It's pink," Billie said. "Very, very pink."

"It's also very weird," Asher said. "I never thought of an old shopping mall as a potential bed and breakfast."

"Well, I am not sure how much 'breakfast' there will be," Billie said.

"I thought there was a cafeteria or something downstairs," Asher said.

"There's some sort of breakfast bar down there," she said. "I haven't been to check anything out just yet."

"Oh, I should tell you that Waffles says hi," Asher said.

"Oh, he told you that himself, did he?" Billie chuckled.

"I took him for a walk this morning and he filled me in on a lot of different things," Asher said.

"I bet he talked you into letting him off the leash," Billie said. Waffles, her stubborn Tibetan Mastiff, had a way of trying to get his way during their walks on the beach. Aside from a remote place on the far southern tip of the island, Billie almost never let him off his leash. He had the compulsion to take off for any clump of seaweed that had washed ashore. More than once, Billie had dragged him home only to pull out the hose and spray him off before pushing him back into his dog pen.

"I let him off for a little while," Asher admitted. "He ran straight for the water's edge and found some seaweed I hadn't even noticed before."

"How hard was it to get him back home?" Billie asked.

Asher answered with a sigh. "We're on the deck of my houseboat, if that tells you anything."

Billie laughed. "It tells me everything I need to know," she said. She didn't have to ask whether he was going to the commissary kitchen later or not. They were heading into the weekend, and while there was no event on the books for the grounds over the weekend, her food truck managers stayed busy just parked in their normal spaces on the boardwalk close to the beach.

Of course, there were three truck managers who would not be utilizing the kitchen. As part of the convention, Billie had arranged for three of her food trucks to accompany her to the mall area. The trucks would be set up with about twenty others in the large parking lot on the south side. An unrelated street fair was scheduled for the same weekend. Convention presenters had been invited to set up their street food trucks nearby.

Billie invited Marcel Johnson and Enid Greene to accompany her to the convention. She reasoned that Marcel's taco truck and Enid's mousse truck would represent different varieties of food. Billie also decided to make the debut of her newest truck at the convention. The truck had been delivered to the commissary kitchen two days before by her island truck renovator, Nolan Wiggins.

The new truck manager had arrived then as well. Lucas Hibberd graduated from the culinary school on the mainland more than ten years ago and came highly recommended from Alex Regent, the attorney who managed her late grandmother's estate. Before a decline in the economy had forced him to close, Lucas had owned a small street food fleet of his own. He excitedly accepted the position as her bratwurst truck manager the second it was offered to him. He arrived on the island with a stack of menus already printed up to hand out to patrons from the food truck. Billie had expressed her glee to Asher.

"He is so prepared," she'd gushed. "I think he is going to be great."

Billie walked out of the bedroom space and went toward the back of the room. She was eager to check out the bathroom and the small kitchen area before she headed out again. Lucas was due to meet her in another hour, so she only had a little time for herself. Billie had arranged to meet with each of the food truck managers outside in the parking lot where their trucks were parked. She intended to sample some of Lucas's menu offerings then, and to introduce him formally to Marcel and Enid. She was curious to hear about their accommodations as well. Enid had booked a room in the mall on the other side and Marcel had opted for a motel room down the road.

She was nervous for her presentation, but excited for the experience as a whole, both for herself and her managers.

CHAPTER 2

"Did you notice the lights in the hallway?" Enid asked when they stood outside between her bakery mousse truck and the bratwurst truck. "I think the place looks kinda creepy."

"It's neat but I guess it is a little weird," Billie said. Despite how fun it might have sounded to her at age thirteen, hanging around an empty shopping mall was a little creepy. "I'm glad the space I rented is small."

"It's not very big?" Marcel asked her. "I'm surprised."

Billie shook her head. "It's about as big as one of those bulk candy stores with the big bins set up around the middle," she said. "I have a bathroom of my own, and that's really all I care about at this point."

"Oh, yeah," Enid said and made a face. "Can you imagine walking around that place at night looking for a bathroom?"

"My mind has already gone there." Billie chuckled. "Nope. Not for me." She looked up to see Lucas approaching from the back of the taco truck. He was taller than Marcel with dark hair and eyes.

"Good morning, everyone," Lucas said. He approached Enid and held out his hands. "Lucas Hibberd, bratwurst truck manager."

"I'm Enid and that's Marcel," Enid said.

"Let me guess," Lucas said. He released her hand and pointed to Marcel, then turned back to her. "Taco truck, cupcake truck."

"Close," Enid said with a smile. "Taco truck, but I run the bakery mousse truck. Still technically cupcakes, but only for convenience's sake."

"I have to say, I was shocked when Billie announced the latest truck," Marcel said. "All I could think about was hot dogs. Aside from ketchup, mustard, and relish, what is there? I mean, I get it now. Especially after I saw the menu you planned, but I was a little confused at first."

Lucas laughed and clapped his hand on the back

of Marcel's shoulder. "Trust me," he said. "I under-stand. You have to open your mind to a whole new world."

"Do you really prepare the brats yourself?" Enid asked.

Lucas smiled and nodded his head. "Every day I will prepare them fresh before I open the truck," he said.

"That's a lot of work in one day," Marcel said.

"It sure sounds like it is, but you would be surprised how fast it goes," Lucas said. "I have a few methods to my madness."

"Speaking of madness," Enid said, turning to Billie. "When is your speech tomorrow?"

"Just before lunch," Billie said.

"Are you nervous?"

Billie smiled. "I am," she said. "I'm still not sure why they asked me to be here, but it's a good oppor-tunity for networking. Plus, you guys get the chance to come here to the mainland and show your trucks off to a new crowd of people. It's good for me, good for the trucks, and good for Sea Glass Island tourism."

"Now I see why," Enid said with a wink. "You're trying out for a job as the head of island tourism."

"Is Rhonda retiring?" Marcel replied.

"Who is Rhonda?" Lucas asked.

"She essentially runs all things tourism related on the island," Billie said. "She was also a close friend of my grandmother's."

"And now she's essentially your mom," Enid said. She poked Billie with her elbow in the ribs.

"That's true." Billie smiled.

"Is that how you got here today, Billie?" Marcel asked. "Did Rhonda drive you off of the island?"

"She did drive me, and Asher is coming Sunday night to pick me up."

Lucas listened with interest. "Do a lot of people on the island go without cars of their own?"

"Oh, she has a car," Enid said.

"I do," Billie said. "I have a car."

"Why do I feel like I am missing an entire section of information?" Lucas asked.

"Because you are," Marcel said. "Billie is sort of infamous for her inability to drive off of the island."

"Or onto it," Enid said.

"But you have a car," Lucas said.

"I do. I drive it all over Sea Glass Island," Billie said.

"And here on the mainland, if she can get it towed over here," Marcel added with a smirk.

"Again with the missing information." Lucas shook his head. "How did you get the car on the island?"

"Tow truck," Billie said.

"She almost drove it herself," Enid added.

"Yeah, I made it about ten seconds on the bridge, and then I stopped in the middle of the road and put it in reverse."

"Okay," Lucas said. "I think I'm getting a clearer picture. You're scared to drive over the bridge."

Billie grinned and nodded her head. "You absolutely have the picture," she said. "The question is, how well do you think you're going to fit in with a bunch of weirdos like us?"

"Oh, I think you could describe the fit like hand and glove," Lucas said. "Do you want to join me at the truck? I have a full menu ready to go for you guys."

"Lead the way," Billie said. She followed Marcel and Lucas around the front of the *Fun in a Bun* truck.

Billie looked over the menu board. She had learned that in the food truck business, less is sometimes more. Lucas offered four bratwurst varieties and a burger made from ground bratwurst meat. Billie wanted to order one of each of the brats but settled on the pear and bacon variety. Marcel chose a beer bratwurst and Enid decided on the Ruben brat. Lucas set out two brat burgers and cut them in half for everyone to sample.

"I want to try some of that German potato salad, too," Billie said. She wasn't the biggest fan of coleslaw, but the sample he had given her two days before was better than she had ever tried. She bit into the pear and bacon bratwurst. Her eyes widened.

"You like that one?" Lucas asked. "I like the contrasting flavors myself."

"The beer brat tastes a lot like a stout German beer," Marcel said.

"That's great since I make it with stout German beer."

After lunch, Billie left her truck managers to their own devices and headed back toward the other side of the mall parking lot. Lincoln told her she could enter and exit through any of the mall doors. Billie decided not to traipse back across the parking lot and head inside. If she had to walk that far, she preferred to walk indoors. Asphalt did not feel good under her feet after living on an island for as long as she had.

Billie slid her room key through the card reader on the nearest entrance and waited for the green light before she pulled the door open. She walked through the small vestibule and pushed open the next door. She went inside and passed two storefronts across the wide hall from each other. "I think I found the mall ghost town," she muttered.

"I'm sorry, dear." A woman stepped in front of her when she rounded the corner. "Did you say something?"

Billie stopped in her tracks. The woman was tall and blonde with a tinge of gray above her ears. She smiled down at her, much like an accommodating elementary school teacher.

"Oh, I was just saying how this is the mall ghost town," Billie said and gestured at the area behind her. "At least, it seems to be now. I don't think this area has been converted to rooms or anything."

The woman nodded. "It was like that back when this was still a bustling retail mecca," she said. "I'm Debra Millstead, by the way."

"Billie Halifax."

"Oh, you're giving the address on street food vending, right?" Debra asked. She smiled and held her hand out to Billie.

Billie nodded and shook the woman's hand. "I'm not sure why they asked me to speak, but yes. That's me."

"Well, if I know anything about the people organizing this convention, they did their research before they picked you for it," Debra said. "So, you ought to take that as a compliment."

"You're the keynote speaker, aren't you?" Billie asked.

Debra smiled and nodded. "I don't know if that was some sort of attempt to lower my prices for hosting their event or not, but they did ask me to fill the keynote spot."

"I don't know," Billie said. "From the glowing review Lincoln Mathers gave you when I met him this morning, it sounds like the keynote spot is right where you belong."

Debra's face instantly fell. "Lincoln Mathers spoke about me this morning?"

Billie nodded her head quickly. "He said that you turned the mall around and transitioned it into a new business when other malls around this area were closing down entirely," she said. "He said you were the one who encouraged him and other store owners to look into the possibility of turning their spaces into overnight rooms."

Debra nodded her head. "A handful of them actually owned their retail spaces. So, I had to get them all on board or else none of this would work."

"Do you consider it a success?" Billie asked.

Debra looked around her and shrugged. "The doors are still open, and the lights are on," she said. "None of us have lost our homes. I guess that means we're successful enough."

"I think that's a good indication," Billie said. "Anyway, it was nice to meet you."

"Where are you staying?" Debra asked.

"Where the Italian charm bracelet store used to be," Billie said. "I'm afraid I don't know a better way to describe it."

Debra smiled. "I know just where you are talking about," she said. "He's done a nice job with that space."

"I agree," Billie said. "There is a lot of pink, though."

"Yes, there is a lot of pink in there," Debra said. "Anyway, it was really nice to chat with you before the convention."

"You as well," Billie said. She walked past Debra toward the middle of the mall. She was shocked again at the expanse of the place. It was set up like a figure eight and she was on the bottom at the far end. To get back to her room for the night, she had to walk all the way around the center and clear around the other side.

As she walked, she passed a few more people and nodded politely. No one stopped to chat with her, and she didn't mind one bit. She had the afternoon and the evening to put the finishing touches on her speech. Her intention was to remain in her room for the evening, and she planned to do just that.

CHAPTER 3

Billie woke early the next morning surrounded by an odd glow of pink. It was a strange thing to wake up to given that there was no natural light in the entire space. Her feet hit the floor and she sighed. Maybe it was a silly thing, but she missed the feel of her own bedroom floor and the cozy cabin-like atmosphere behind the sliding barn door in her own tiny house. She also missed the sound of the waves crashing against the shore when she left her window open for the night.

Maybe most of all, she missed the low impact walk she took with Waffles every morning on the soft white sand, but this a temporary arrangement. The invitation to speak at a business convention meant she was recognized for doing something right, at least, she thought. Her hope was that she would learn from the others when they spoke.

The chance to expose the food trucks to more people on the mainland was something she couldn't pass up. On the island, the food trucks down on the boardwalk had become such a staple, it was the first place tourists were directed for a good meal. The fact that there were other restaurants on the far side of the island made no difference. She had heard rumors that some people traveled over the bridge on the weekends just to visit their favorite food truck, but she wasn't sure just how truthful that was. Either way, the carnival going on at the same time as the business convention provided an unparalleled chance to expose the trucks to the general public.

After a fast shower, Billie dressed quickly in her light blue pantsuit and reviewed her speech while her hair dried. In just a few hours she would stand before a group of at least one hundred other small business owners and deliver it. She wanted to make sure she knew the words well enough that she could look out over the crowd. The last thing she wanted was to stand up in front of the room full of professionals and read from a piece of paper like a second grader giving a speech at school.

Although, when she held the speech in her shaking hands, she felt a lot like a second grader. She fought to get over herself and read over the speech for a full hour before she returned to the bathroom to finish getting ready. One more glance in the mirror and Billie told herself that she had done everything she possibly could do.

She sat back down for a second to review the speech again, then set it to the side. There was such a thing as going over it too much, she decided. If she was going to make it through the day, coffee was a necessity. Billie slipped her shoes on and swiped her room key off the small table next to the bed. She pulled her cell phone off the charger and carried it with her out the door.

As soon as the door closed behind her, the aroma of bacon and coffee hit her. She could hear the din of voices coming from the level below her. She walked around the long curve toward the escalator in the center of the figure eight and headed downstairs for breakfast.

"Good morning, Billie," Enid called out to her as soon as she stepped off the escalator. Billie waved and looked around. Like most things in the converted mall, the eating area was arranged in the middle of a much larger space. Billie felt like she was out in the middle of the ocean on a small island when she walked toward the counter to order her breakfast. Several dozen people easily fit in the tables and chairs set up in the seating area, but another two or three hundred were needed to fill up the cavernous space. Billie tried to shrug off the almost eerie feeling the place gave her.

"How did you sleep?" she asked Enid when she carried her tray of food over and took a seat next to her.

"Well," Enid said, looking around. "Everything was comfortable and nice, but I have to admit the space is so big I feel almost lost in it. It's weird being in an old mall."

"I second that," Lucas whispered, leaning over. "Like she said, the place is fine. Nice mattress and comfy pillows, but it does feel weird when you can hear the echo of your own breathing when you're trying to go to sleep."

"This place seems popular enough, though," Billie said. She picked up her coffee and closed her eyes with the first sip. "Lincoln told me that turning the mall store spaces into rentals was Debra's idea."

"Who is that?" Enid asked. She looked over the top of Billie's head.

"Who is who?" Marcel asked.

Billie turned her head and spotted a silver-haired man coming down the escalator. He was dressed in a steel gray three-piece suit. He exhaled when he stepped off of the escalator and smiled at the crowd.

"Good morning, convention attendees," he sang out. He hesitated for a moment before he spoke again, as if he expected a response to his greeting. When no one said anything in return, his smile widened. "I am Calvin Greer, organizer of this weekend's event." Polite applause followed.

"Welcome, Calvin," Lincoln Mathers called out from the other side of the space, close to the breakfast counter. A murmur of voices followed his lead.

"And here she is now," Calvin called out. He began clapping loudly, gesturing toward the escalator on the other side of the mall. Debra Millstead appeared at the top and rode it down. "Our keynote speaker and owner of this mall, Debra Millstead." A few people turned their heads and clapped.

Billie applauded as well as she looked around the room. Several people nodded their heads and smiled. Calvin Greer's mouth froze, more of a grimace than a smile, she observed. She looked around the room where she had seen Lincoln Mathers a moment before, but only saw his back as he walked out of the space.

"Thank you," Debra said as she walked into the eating area. "Thank you, everyone." She smiled awkwardly as she approached the breakfast counter. Billie wondered if the attention bothered her.

There was a long pause. Calvin Greer remained in his spot near the escalator while Debra filled her plate and accepted a tall mug of coffee from the person behind the counter. Billie glanced at her own Styrofoam cup and immediately wished she had brought her own ceramic mug from home.

"I'm terrible," she muttered.

"Why do you say that?" Lucas asked.

"Because I saw the server hand the owner of the mall her coffee in a real coffee cup and now, I am missing my own cups back home," Billie said.

Lucas stared at her for a long moment, as if he was unsure whether she was joking or not. He then rose and made his way over to the counter where he leaned in and asked the server a question.

"What is he doing?" Enid asked.

"I'm afraid I know," Billie said. She ducked her head in embarrassment. Lucas lingered at the counter for a few moments longer, then returned to their table empty-handed.

"I'm afraid the mall does not furnish reusable coffee mugs to guests," Lucas said.

Billie sighed. "I appreciate your efforts, but I really didn't need a mug. I was just missing my own creature comforts."

"You're out of your comfort zone here, aren't you?" Enid asked.

Billie popped a bite of her eggs in her mouth and nodded her head. "You have no idea," she said. "I have less than two hours to get my act together."

"Are you prepared?" Marcel asked her. "You know we'll all be in the audience, right?"

Billie shook her head. "No, I did not know that," she said. "I just assumed you would all be busy in your food trucks."

Enid shook her head. "We've all decided to postpone opening by an hour just so we can attend your lecture."

Billie was surprised and began to form her words of gratitude in her head. She was just about to open her mouth to speak when a scream rang out across the entire lower level. Billie and a few others stood up immediately and searched for the source.

"Debra! Someone help her!" The shout came from the far side of the seating area. Billie swiveled her head and looked around. A group of people swarmed around a table on the far end of the area where Debra Millstead had been seated. Billie pushed her chair back and headed in the general direction. She stood about fifteen feet from her table. She saw Debra Millstead lying face down on the table. She immediately pulled her phone out of her pocket and dialed the police.

CHAPTER 4

"You can't force us all to stay here," a woman shouted at the police officers standing in front of the breakfast counter. They were gathered in small groups all over the lower level of the mall. Four uniformed officers stood around the table where Debra remained face down on the table.

"When are you going to move her out of here?" another voice called out. "She is clearly expired. If we can't leave, at least call the coroner, and have her removed."

Billie exchanged looks with Enid, who was still seated across the table from her. Marcel and Lucas had been moved across the room. Each was seated at a small table facing a police officer. Billie figured the two of them were next. Maybe the one-by-one questioning meant they could leave the mall sooner. She had already decided to head back to her home on Sea Glass Island, even if she had to walk all the way there.

There was little doubt in her mind that the convention would be canceled, especially since the owner of the venue had just been murdered right in front of the convention attendees. Billie was already sure Debra's death had been deliberate, even if the actual cause of death had not been announced yet. It was too convenient that her death took place in front of a large crowd of people. Billie's instincts told her that the point was either to complicate the investigation into who was responsible, or it might have been more of a deliberate statement.

If she was right and the second assumption was true, finding the killer was even more urgent. She worried there might have been an element of revenge in the death. If that was the case, the killing might not be over.

"Okay, you and you." A police officer approached their table and pointed her finger at Billie and Enid.

She nodded to Billie. "You're with me, and you can head over there with Officer Rogers."

Enid stood and walked toward the male officer on the other side of the group of tables. Billie followed the female officer to another table that had been placed close to the escalators.

"Have a seat," the officer said when they reached the table. Billie carefully pulled out the chair and slid down in it. She folded her hands on the table and waited for the officer to take her seat.

"Name?"

"Billie Halifax," she said quickly.

"Okay, and you're one of the featured speakers for this conference, correct?"

Billie nodded her head. "I was supposed to talk about maintaining my food truck fleet," she offered. "Three of the trucks out in the parking lot are part of my fleet."

"Good to know," the officer said. "Any reason why you're being so helpful with the unnecessary information?"

Billie shrugged her shoulders. "Why wouldn't I be?" she asked. "You have a job to do and the faster I do my part to help you get it done, the faster I get to leave this place. Same thing goes for my food truck managers."

"You said there are three of them here with you?" the officer asked.

"No, I didn't say, but yes," Billie said. "Three of them are here. Do you want their names?"

"Sure. Why don't you give me their names and tell me which trucks they run."

Billie nodded. "Lucas Hibberd is the man you were just talking to before me, and he's the manager of the bratwurst truck. Marcel Johnson is my taco truck manager. The last one is the other woman you sent over there to the other officer. Her name is Enid Greene, and she runs my mousse truck."

The officer's eyes grew wide. "You serve moose? Like, moose from Alaska?"

Billie chuckled and shook her head. "No, mousse, like chocolate mousse, the kind you get in the middle of a wedding cake. It's a dessert truck. She mostly serves mousse filled cupcakes of various flavors."

"Oh, I was going to ask you a whole lot of other questions," the officer said. "Anyway, I assume you were all seated at the table where I just found you and you were all there the entire time?"

"No, the three of them were seated together when I came down here from my room about forty-five minutes ago," Billie said. "Lucas had gotten up and gone over to the breakfast bar a few minutes before the scream came."

"Lucas did? Did he walk past Debra Millstead's table?"

"Not even close to it," Billie said.

"Why did he go to the breakfast bar?" the officer asked. "From what I saw, most of the food on your plates was gone. Did he just walk over there for the fun of it or was he still hungry?"

"No," Billie said carefully. "I had said something about wishing I had one of my coffee mugs from home and he got up and walked over there and asked for one."

"Just like that, he got up to get you what you wanted at that exact moment?" the officer asked. Billie noticed the name on her shirt for the first time. Burke.

"I didn't expect him to do it, but yes. He just got up and walked over there and asked. He came right back to the table and nothing else weird happened."

"Is it weird that he went to the breakfast bar for you?" Officer Burke asked. "Are the two of you a romantic item?

"Oh, no, no," Billie said, shaking her head. "He just arrived on the island a couple of days ago. Brand new food truck manager."

"Oh, so you hardly know him," Officer Burke said. "What was he doing, trying to impress you?"

"I have no idea," Billie replied. "If I had to guess, I would say he was just trying to be a nice guy."

"Okay, Miss Halifax," Officer Burke said. "Is

there anything else you can tell me about what took place right before the victim died?"

Billie sighed. She had observed a few things, but she was reluctant to share them, given the officer's suspicious nature and tone of voice. "Okay, the reason I thought about my own coffee mugs at home was because Debra was served her coffee in a ceramic mug, a tall one. Seeing that made me think of what I'm used to at home.

"And this is relevant how, exactly?" Officer Burke asked.

"I honestly don't know whether it's relevant or not, but it seems like an important detail for you to know if the cause of death was delivered by what she ate or drank," Billie said.

"Okay, that's actually very astute of you to point out," the officer said. "Anything else?"

"Well, I thought it was strange that the convention organizer, Calvin Greer, called out Debra Millstead when she came down the back escalator. He treated her like a celebrity and called for applause for her," Billie said. "He acted like a celebrity himself when he came down the other escalator."

"Why do you think that's strange?"

"I wouldn't have thought much about it if she hadn't died a short time after he did it," Billie said.

"Again, why does it seem strange to you?"

"I don't know. It just stands out to me," Billie said. "His entrance was odd. I don't really know how else to say it, but it was odd."

"Okay, just a couple more questions for you and then you can go back to your room," Officer Burke said.

"Back to my room? We can't leave?"

Officer Burke shook her head slowly. "Yeah, afraid nobody is going to be leaving here for a while," she said. "This place is huge. It's going to take us a while to conduct a search, let alone process interviews."

"That makes sense, but I'm eager to get back to my home and my other businesses," Billie said.

"I understand, but unfortunately, it's not going to work that way. Right now, I need to know if you'd met Debra before today."

Billie nodded. "I met her yesterday afternoon," she said. "I was coming back through the mall after visiting with my food truck managers over in the side parking lot. I said something out loud about finding the ghost town part of the mall and she overheard me. We spoke for a few minutes and then we went our separate ways."

"What did you speak about?" Officer Burke

asked.

"What we were speaking on for the convention," Billie said. "We also talked about Lincoln Mathers, the man I'm renting my room from. He's the one who told me about Debra and how she pivoted this place when the rest of the malls in the area shut down. He gave her a lot of credit for reinventing everything. That alone is an excellent lesson in business."

"I see. My other question is, did you have anything against Debra Millstead?"

"I only just met her," Billie said. "I mean, I was looking forward to her keynote speech, but I was more familiar with the content of the description of her address than I was with her."

"Okay," Officer Burke said. She stood up and pushed her chair in. "That's all I need from you for right now. Don't leave the mall until further notice."

Billie nodded and walked slowly back to her table. She took a seat next to Marcel and sighed. "We can't leave for the time being," she said quietly.

Marcel nodded. "That's what they said to me as well," he said. "I don't think that's going to go over very well. There are over a hundred people here. How are you going to tell them that they can't leave?"

Billie shook her head. "I don't know, but hopefully it's only for a few hours."

CHAPTER 5

"I need your attention, please." Billie turned around in her seat and stared at another new face. Each of the uniformed officers turned toward the man dressed in a white shirt and tie. His badge hung from a chain around his neck. "Ladies and gentlemen, I'm Detective Jim Collins. As you are all aware, we are investigating the events that occurred. I'm sure that each of you is wary of sitting here and waiting while we take your statements, but I am also aware that this death occurred in a room full of people. These are not normal circumstances."

"Are there ever normal circumstances in murders?" Billie asked under her breath. Enid snickered next to her.

"As I was saying," Detective Collins said, staring

in their direction. "Due to these unusual circum-stances, I'm afraid that we are going to have to prevail upon your patience for a little while longer. You are all excused from this general area, but do not leave the mall itself."

Audible groans filled the room. "Why can't we leave?" someone shouted.

"I think I just explained that very clearly," Detec-tive Collins said.

"What if I call my attorney?" another woman asked.

"Call your attorney," Detective Collins said. "They can arrange for your bail because that's the alternative. Either we detain all of you right here, or I read you your rights as a group and we start making arrests. Everyone here is a potential suspect. Got that? You are all under suspicion. Nobody leaves. If you try to leave, the next step is a night in the county jail."

"You can't do that," a man stood up and yelled. He raised his fist in the air and shook it at the detective.

"Rogers? Burke?" The detective nodded toward his officers. They swiftly surrounded the man and placed him in handcuffs.

"Anyone else?" Detective Collins looked over the crowd. "Alright, thank you for your understanding. I will be placing officers outside every exit until you are all released to leave. Right now, I suggest you return to your rooms and hang out. I believe there still is a P.A. system in this place. Listen for updates and announcements."

"Detective?" A woman raised her hand in the middle of the room. "Please, sir. I don't want to go to jail, but I have a question. Some of us have not rented rooms here. I'm booked at a hotel down the road."

Detective Collins gave her a smug grin and shook his head slowly. "I don't know what to tell you, ma'am. Find a couch and take a nap," he said. "And if it isn't obvious to the rest of you, the conference has been canceled."

Billie stood up and waited while her truck managers gathered around her. They walked together toward the escalator and rode it up to the next level. "Marcel, you aren't booked here either."

Marcel shook his head. "Nope," he said.

"I know we just met, but you can hang in my room with me, dude," Lucas offered.

"That's nice of you, man," Marcel said. Billie could read the concern on his face.

"Miss Halifax," Lincoln Mathers called to her when they made it to the top level. He walked toward the four of them. "I just heard the announcement from the police. I want to let you know that there is a room behind yours available if any of your employees need it. I won't charge you any extra for the use of it."

Billie sighed in relief. She didn't distrust Lucas personally, but she did not know him. Given the circumstances they were facing, she didn't want to push Marcel to room with a stranger.

"That's wonderful, Mr. Mathers," she said. "We'd really appreciate that."

"Okay, why don't you follow me, and we'll get everything set up," he said.

Billie glanced at Marcel. He nodded in her direction and followed behind Lincoln. Billie glanced at Enid and Lucas. "You guys should go relax for a little while. Stay in touch by text," she said.

Enid squeezed her arm and walked in the direction of her room. Lucas nodded and took off the other way.

Billie waited while Lincoln situated Marcel in his room. She stood to the side while Lincoln showed him the room and handed over the room key. She walked with Lincoln back toward her own room. "Mr. Mathers, do you know if there are security cameras in the parking lot? I'm going to assume that my food truck managers are not going to have access to their trucks until we're released by the police. I'm worried about those trucks taking off somewhere if you get my meaning."

Lincoln frowned. "I'm afraid there are no working cameras on the premises any longer," he said. "Budget doesn't allow for it."

Billie sighed. "I was afraid of that," she said. "I'm not sure if I can have them driven back to the island where we're from or not."

"That might be a question for the police themselves," Lincoln said. "I don't know why you couldn't have the police escort your managers to the trucks and have them park in the back. There are several loading docks and enough room for multiple semi-trucks. Surely there would be room enough for a few food trucks."

"Thank you," Billie said. "I think that's something I'll ask Officer Burke as soon as I can find her. Maybe it's silly, but with the carnival going on in the next block, I don't trust my food trucks to be safe, especially since we have no idea how long we'll be here."

"Yes, and the carnival will be going on all night. I wouldn't want my trucks left out there unattended, either," Lincoln said. "Not to mention, not all the food trucks over there are owned by convention attendees. Some are just regular street food vendors, and they'll be open. To me, that makes the trucks that aren't open even more vulnerable."

Billie thanked him again for his help and headed back to her own room. She slid her key in the reader and waited for it to open. As soon as she was inside, she closed the door behind her and pulled out her phone. She dialed Asher's number right away and waited until the voicemail recording started. She ended the phone call without leaving a message and sent a brief text instead. Next, she sent a group message to Enid, Marcel, and Lucas.

"I'm going to check with the police about having the trucks moved around to the back of the mall and away from the parking lot next to the carnival," she wrote. "That way we can keep an eye on them. Please stand by."

Billie changed out of her pantsuit and back into her jeans. Since the convention had been canceled, there was no need to trudge around in her fancy clothes and shoes. She was more interested in comfort at the moment. She headed back out into the mall and down to the lower level where she immediately searched for the police officer that had questioned her before.

"Can I help you?" one of the officers stopped to ask.

Billie nodded her head. "I gave my statement to Officer Burke earlier," she said. "I wondered if I could speak to her again."

"Is there something I can help you with?" the officer asked.

Billie nodded and smiled. "I hope so, though I hate to bother you with this," she said. "I'm the owner of three of those food trucks parked outside in the far parking lot. I wondered if there was any way I could have my truck managers move the trucks to the rear of the mall where the delivery bays are located. That way they can be away from the carnival traffic."

"Ma'am, I don't know if we can arrange that," the officer said.

"Arrange what?" Detective Collins asked from behind her. Billie turned around to face him.

"This woman has a request about her vehicle," the officer said.

"Detective, I was just making an inquiry about moving my three food trucks to the back of the mall. I have three truck managers in attendance here with me and as long as we are all detained inside, there will be no one to keep a watch over the trucks."

"Is there anything valuable inside these trucks?" the detective asked with a smirk.

"As a matter of fact, yes," Billie shot back. "Not

only are the trucks self-contained businesses, each one is furnished with state of the art equipment and inventory. Each one has a cash drawer in it as well, and without seeing for myself, I'm unaware how much cash there is in each one. The carnival going on next to the mall parking lot is expected to run all night and since no one can tell us how long we'll be here, I'd like to keep my property as safe as possible."

"I am well aware of what is going on in the next lot," Detective Collins said.

"Then you must be aware that three empty food trucks pose an attractive nuisance for troublemakers," she said. "My trucks come fully insured, but I don't want the hassle of making a claim on each one of them. As soon as this conference is over, each one of those trucks will return to Sea Glass Island and continue to operate like they do every day. Losing even one of them is a substantial loss for my business, not to mention the managers who maintain them."

"Are your trucks stocked up for the day? I mean, is there food available on them right now?"

Billie nodded her head. "Yes, for the day," she said. "But for tomorrow the managers were going to run back to the island for more supplies if need be."

Detective Collins nodded. "I assume there might

be enough food on each of these trucks to feed around a hundred to a hundred and fifty people?"

"Easily," Billie said. "Although one of the trucks is a dessert truck."

"That works," he said. "Here is what we're going to do: Your managers can walk with an officer across the parking lot and drive the trucks around to the back of the mall and into the loading bays. You can park the trucks inside the mall close to the doors so the doors can remain open while they prepare dinner for everyone stuck here."

"I'm sorry? You want us to make dinner for everyone here?" she asked.

"Makes sense to me," the detective said. "You get a secure place to stow the trucks overnight and we don't have to try to figure out how to feed all of these people this evening. Of course, you will provide this as a service to us."

"Of course, we can feed you but I'm not sure free is a fair price," Billie said. She wanted to argue that he was asking her to give up thousands of dollars of food for free but felt like she was pushing her luck if she did. As it was she planned to compensate the managers for their time preparing the food.

"Free sounds perfect to me and I assume my officers are welcome to eat for free as well."

Billie sighed. "Can I have my managers come and meet with your officers now? I would like to get the trucks moved as soon as possible." She thought it was best to get her trucks moved before arguing her point.

"Is there a rush?" he asked. Billie wanted to point out the audacity in the question given the fact that he had just informed her that she was not only feeding the other convention attendees for free, but the entire police department as well.

"The carnival is under way now. By lunchtime the crowd around the street food area will be significant," she said. "I would prefer that the trucks be moved before the crowd grows that large."

"Okay. That's fair," the detective said. "Summon the managers. Have them meet us on the far side of the mall near the door that leads to the parking lot. I will send out three officers and you can walk with me to oversee it."

Billie nodded and pulled her phone out of her pocket. She sent a text to each of them with the instructions the detective gave her. Each one responded immediately. "They are on their way now," she said.

"Shall we?" Detective Collins asked her.

CHAPTER 6

Detective Collins held the door for her. Billie walked past him and out onto the sidewalk. She watched as Marcel, Enid, and Lucas walked side by side with police officers to the parking spaces where their trucks were parked.

"What trucks do you have back on Sea Glass Island?" Detective Collins asked her.

"I have two other dessert trucks, ice cream and cupcakes specifically," she said. "And in addition to the taco and bratwurst trucks, we also have a vegan truck."

"Oh, vegan? Not for me," the detective said. "What else?"

"Pizza, barbecue, sushi, and burgers," she said. She was not in the mood for small talk with the man.

"It sounds like you're quite a success," Detective Collins said. "You were here to speak about those successes?"

"I was here to talk about my business, Detective," Billie said. "I already gave my statement to Officer Burke."

"Oh, was I interrogating you?" he asked her. "I thought we were just having a conversation here, but since you think I'm still questioning you, what can you tell me about Lucas Hibberd?"

"Lucas? I am afraid I don't know a whole lot about him," Billie said. "He just came to work for me a couple of days ago. I can tell you that he is a highly skilled chef with an impressive resume. He isn't a brand-new graduate from culinary school either. He ran a successful food truck business himself for a while."

"How did he take the loss of his business? Would you characterize him as devastated by that loss?" Detective Collins asked.

Billie stopped walking and shook her head. "I wouldn't know how to answer that question, Detective," she said. "I didn't know him back then. In the short time I have known him, I've never seen anything to indicate that he has any lingering devastation over it."

"But you don't know him well enough to say that he would never hurt anyone," the detective said.

"Are you saying that Lucas is a suspect? He just came here from another state. How would he know the victim well enough to want to harm her?"

"You know, Miss Halifax," he said. "Sometimes you just have to follow the opportunity and the actions and figure out the reason and the motive afterward. Lucas was up and mobile just before Debra Millstead died."

"I hope that's a creative way of saying that you're looking at Lucas because you have nothing else to go with for now," Billie said. "Don't forget that at least hundred people were in the same room. There are dozens of witnesses that can attest to the fact that he never went anywhere near her table."

"Okay, you apparently have given some thought to this," Detective Collins said. "Where do you think I should be looking?" They stood about fifty feet away from the section of the parking lot where the food trucks were parked. Enid started her truck first and carefully backed it up away from the others. Billie spotted a police officer in the cab of the truck with her.

"I suppose that depends on the manner of her death," Billie said. "Immediately I would look at the server who gave her the coffee mug. Maybe whoever prepared the food. I don't know, but that is where I would start."

"And you don't think that's where we have already started?"

"I don't know why you are taking my words as a challenge, Detective Collins," Billie shot back. "I simply answered the questions you asked me."

"Fair enough," he said. He waited while Lucas and then Marcel drove their trucks across the parking lot. They walked across the rest of the way around the far side of the mall. The trucks had disappeared from their sight down the hill and around the back.

"Out of curiosity, how on earth did you ever find yourself in this business?" Detective Collins asked after several minutes of silence.

Billie laughed and shook her head. She wasn't sure she wanted to fill him in on the story, but she was also unsure if she had a choice. Would he find some small nugget of information in her words to use against her? She knew the truth could be proven so she sighed and began.

"I left culinary school just weeks short of graduation," she began. "And I have always regretted that fact."

"Why did you leave?"

"Uh, well, to put it bluntly, family pressures," she said. "My mother wanted me to come and live with her. She has never been one to handle life very well on her own."

"So you went."

Billie nodded. "And so I went," she said. "When you're young and easily manipulated you don't consider the potential consequences to your own future. Anyway, a few years ago when my grand-mother died, she left a large sum of money to me along with a detailed plan to get this business up and running. All I had to do was leave behind a grueling waitressing job at a greasy spoon in the middle of downtown Boston and relocate to an island in the middle of the Gulf of Mexico. It wasn't a hard choice."

"Wow, that is an interesting tale," Detective Collins said. "I don't think I could have come up with that myself."

Billie nodded her head. "It is pretty wild," she said. "And there is an attorney who handles the estate named Alex Regent who can verify everything I just told you. He's located in St. Petersburg, Florida."

Billie cast a last look at the detective and walked quickly ahead of him. She was sick of his constant challenge to every word she said. Before he had the chance to say more, she walked swiftly around the back of the mall. Her feet began to ache and her back hurt. The distance to the loading bays in the back turned out to be much longer than she had expected. By the time she slowed her pace as she approached the first bay where Enid had parked her truck, she was out of breath.

"So, we're making food for all of these people?" Enid asked.

Billie shrugged. "I guess so," she said, not even wanting to argue anymore. "Don't worry about your time. I'll make sure you are compensated for it just like you would be after a normal Friday night on the boardwalk." Since the police department had so easily availed themselves to her food trucks, she was determined not to make her truck managers lose out on income they would have normally had.

"That's kind of you, Billie," Enid said quietly. "But this whole thing stinks, in my opinion."

"You're telling me," Billie said. "I just had the longest walk possible with a police detective."

"How did that go?" Enid asked.

"I'm not sure," Billie said. "I don't know if I was being interrogated the entire time or if that guy is just really bad at small talk. All I know is that I can't wait for all of this to be over."

CHAPTER 7

"What does he expect us to do, exactly?" Marcel asked Billie from the inside of his taco truck. He kept his voice low. The taco truck was parked in a bay between Enid's mousse truck and Lucas' bratwurst truck.

Billie could smell the savory aromas coming from the bratwurst truck. Despite the circumstances, Billie felt a swell of pride for her truck managers. Given the fact that the police department had essentially ordered them to fire up their trucks and work for nothing, each one was inside their trucks preparing food as if they were doing it for royalty. Billie made the rounds between them to offer her help wherever she could.

"I think we're just supposed to cook and serve whatever we can," Billie said.

"I mean, are we taking orders? Or are we just cooking food and setting it out for people to take?" Marcel asked.

"I think we just make it simple," Billie said. "We'll set out the fixings and let everyone assemble their own tacos. I'm going to tell Lucas to do the same thing for his truck."

"Sounds good to me," Marcel said. "Because I have to admit that I do not possess the patience to stand here and make things to order for a crowd of people who aren't paying for it and aren't even pretending to be thankful."

"Marcel," Billie said. "I'm completely behind you, but I do want you to know that you and the others will be compensated for today. I'm going to pay you what you would have made on the boardwalk."

"That's very generous of you," Marcel said. "But this police department ought to be doing that. They should at least offer to pay for the food. I can't imagine Detective Sullivan or Chief Abernathy back home ordering a private business to furnish the food and the labor to prepare it for an entire group of people."

"Is there a problem here?" Detective Collins

asked. He poked his head inside the open order window.

"A problem? There is no problem," Marcel asked. "We were just talking."

"You were talking about my department," he said.

"I was speaking to my boss about how we are going to handle your request that we feed everyone here," Marcel said. "And your department."

Billie nodded. "He's right, Detective," she said. "We were just discussing how we planned to do it. I told Marcel I don't think it's necessary to take custom orders. Under these circumstances, I want to keep it simple and allow the diners to fix their own tacos at the very least."

"How would you handle a group of customers on the beach?" Detective Collins asked, nodding at Marcel. "I assume you serve food to people on the beach where you're from."

Billie eyed the detective closely. He was a difficult man to read. Her instincts told her he was a hard man, in general. "He would take orders," she said. "But these are not typical circumstances, and we are not on the beach."

"You are still a food truck," Detective Collins said. He pointed his index finger directly at Marcel. "Open up this window and take orders like each and every one of these people were paying you top dollar for the food you're preparing. You make everything to order."

"And if I don't?" A defiant Marcel stood in the middle of his kitchen with his hands on his hips.

"If you don't, I'm going to throw you in handcuffs so fast you won't know what hit you," Detective Collins said. His upper lip snarled as he spoke. He turned to Billie next. "And this food truck will be confiscated and thrown into the impound lot so fast the grill will sizzle while they tow it away. You can bet that it will be years before you ever see it again. So, you better get your act together and start making food the way I told you to do it."

"Detective Collins, you can't force us…"

"Oh yeah? You watch me," he said to Billie. "I'll show you what the real world is like out here for people without silver spoons in their mouths."

"Who has a silver spoon?" Marcel asked him. "I work my fingers to the bone to earn the living I do."

"I'm not talking about you," the detective said. "I mean your boss here. She's the one who was given a fleet of food trucks, right?"

Lincoln Mathers appeared outside in the truck bay. "Detective," he said, clearing his throat loudly. "Can I have a word with you, please?"

"I'm kind of in the middle of something right now," Detective Collins snapped.

"I'm afraid this won't wait, Detective," Lincoln repeated. He nodded briefly at Billie and waited outside with his hands hooked together behind his back.

"Fine," Detective Collins said. He walked toward Lincoln but turned back briefly. "You better do it the way I told you."

"Now, please," Lincoln snapped under his breath. Billie heard the comment as the pair walked inside the receiving area of the mall.

"What in the world was that all about?" Enid asked. She stood in the doorway to the food truck with Lucas right behind her.

"I don't know, but I think I need to step away for a minute and call my lawyer," Billie announced. "This isn't right. I know this isn't right."

"I agree," Lucas said. He leaned over Enid's shoulder and spoke quietly. "Something is off with that detective. I can't put my finger on it, but something is off with that guy."

Billie agreed with Lucas wholeheartedly, but she could do no more than that. She reassured her crew that she would return as fast as she could. For now, she told them, it would be better to just do what the angry detective told them to do. She hoped that the man would be quickly put in his place, however.

She walked quickly through the receiving bays. Guided only by ambient light through the vast, empty inventory area, Billie made her way toward the glowing exit sign several hundred feet in the distance. As she walked, she checked her phone for service. Nothing. She walked a little faster. The deeper she walked into the belly of the warehouse, the more she felt panic nagging at her.

Billie slowly jogged to the door under the exit sign. She pushed it open, hoping that she had reached the retail portion of the mall, but the door led to another darkened room. She could see the light under a door ahead of her, but there were no other lights in the space. She was unsure where she had ended up, perhaps in an unused store or another retail area. Either way, any sense of direction had escaped her.

The distance to the sliver of light seemed to be as far as the exit sign had been when she left the receiving bay, but she couldn't be sure how far she had to go. She was completely surrounded by darkness. If she was in some retail space, chances were that she might wind up colliding with a piece of furniture or a fixture left over from when the mall was a thriving spot. She pulled her phone back out and turned her flashlight on, rolling her eyes at herself for not thinking of it sooner.

Still, the phone's flashlight illuminated the area in front of her just enough to keep her one step ahead of anything that might be in her way. She moved around stacks of chairs, boxes, and a long counter top. But the light only went so far. She was in what felt like a vacuum of darkness.

Billie felt the hair on the back of her neck stand up as she walked. She heard something in the distance and decided that it was an echo of her own footsteps. She walked a little further and stopped when it dawned on her that the footsteps she heard were out of time with her own.

Somehow, she had lost sight of the sliver of light in the distance. She no longer had any sense of direction. More troubling to her at the moment was the fact that the footsteps continued in the distance. She could hear something scooting across the floor, and then voices filled the room. Both were male, though she heard only voices, not the words that they were saying.

Billie turned her phone light off. She was breathing faster as the steps and the voices grew closer. Surrounded by darkness, she fought hard to keep the panic down. Slowly she inhaled through her nose and forced herself to wait a few seconds before she exhaled.

"What was that back there?" one voice said. She could hear the words plainly. Her heart raced at the thought that they were closer.

"What? What did I do?" the other voice asked.

"You know exactly what I'm talking about," the first one said. Billie listened closely to the voices. She was almost certain she recognized at least one of them. She carefully knelt down where she stood and balanced her phone on her leg. She tried to hide the light from the screen as she searched through her phone apps for the voice recorder. She turned the recorder on and hoped it picked up the voices.

"All I did was arrange to have these people fed without us losing any more money," the second voice said.

"No, you basically extorted free meals for more than one hundred people out of that woman and her employees, then you threatened one of them with jail if he didn't do it the way you wanted him to."

"So what?"

Billie was sure she was listening to Detective Collins and another man speaking, but she wasn't sure who. She had seen the detective leave with

Lincoln Mathers, but she wasn't sure if it was his voice or not.

"So what? If you cause any undo trouble for us, that might not bode too well. You need to tone it down. That woman doesn't have any obligation to feed every one of these people out of her own pocket, and definitely not to a group of entitled cops."

"Hey," the second man said. "Who said that my guys are entitled?"

"I do, and you're the worst among them," the first one said.

"Who cares? She's as bad as the rest of them! Did you hear how she got the business she's in? She inherited those food trucks from her grandma," the second man said. "How is she any better than the rest of them? She is no different than that Millstead woman."

Billie fell forward slightly. Her phone flew out of her hand and landed on the floor in front of her. The sound echoed throughout the dark space. Immediately, she went to her knees and began feeling around on the floor for her phone.

"Who's there?" Billie heard Detective Collins shout. "Show yourself now or else."

"Put that away," the first voice hissed in the darkness. "Are you crazy? You don't even know if there was anyone there! Have you seen these rooms? This room alone is probably home to a hundred rats. That could have been anything. But if that gun goes off…"

Before the man could get the words out, a loud crack echoed through the vast space. Billie went straight to the floor and covered her head with her arms. She closed her eyes tightly and did her best not to scream.

"Oh, no," the second voice called out a few minutes later. "No, no, no! Linc! Wake up! Lincoln!" Billie heard shuffling around and more footsteps. The steps stopped. Billie raised her head up slightly. "If there is anyone in here, you better know I will find you. I will not stop looking for you. And when I do, you will wish you were never born."

Billie found her phone again and carefully covered the screen up while she turned the voice recorder off. She pushed the phone deep inside her shirt and folded her hands under her forehead, resting for as long as she could stand to remain still. She could hear the scurrying of something in the distance. The words of the two men came back to her. She did not want to meet any rats in the dark. Several moments had passed, she hoped, since the gun had gone off in the darkness. Her heart continued to race as she stood up.

Billie moved slowly, a step at a time, to her left. She could hear vermin skittering on the other side of the room. Somewhere in the distance she could hear the sound of footsteps, a lot of them moving at once. The sliver of light appeared at last. Billie moved as fast as she could toward the light and hoped that she could enter the main part of the mall unseen.

CHAPTER 8

"What is going on?" Billie whispered to Enid when she caught up with her in the hall. After several more minutes in the darkness, Billie had emerged in a darkened recess of the lower level. She ran into a small group of people swiftly walking toward the food court. Enid, Marcel, and Lucas were among them.

"We have been ordered to return to our rooms," Enid said. "And told that we should not speak to each other."

"By who?" Billie asked.

"By Detective Collins, among others," Enid said. Billie glanced up at the two uniformed officers walking behind the group.

"What's the reason?" Billie whispered.

"Apparently there was another murder," Enid said. "Collins came out and said a body had been found in the warehouse. He said the killer was loose in the middle of the mall and that he had heard them escaping. He chased them down and they got away."

"You two, stop talking," one of the officers snapped behind them. Static crackled over his radio. Billie glanced back toward the officer. He pulled a radio off his belt and listened for a second. "Copy that," he said into the radio. "Okay, everyone hold up here."

"What's going on?" the other officer asked.

"I need everyone to listen," he said. "I have been ordered to collect your cell phones. Come on. Right now. Everyone. Hand over your phones."

"I don't think you can do that," a woman said from the front of the line. "I worked as a paralegal for a number of years. You can't just confiscate private property."

"Really? Is that how you want to answer me?" The officer marched forward and stood directly in front of the woman. "Give me your phone. Now."

The older woman shook her head. "I don't have it with me," she said. Her voice trembled. "I left it in my hotel room."

"That's a load of bull," the officer said. He took a

step closer to the woman. His nose was directly over the top of her head.

"Duane, don't," the other officer said.

"I'm within my rights here. Are you going to listen to me or not?"

"I told you already. I don't have it with me."

"Comply with my orders and give me your phone," he barked.

"Come on, Duane," the other officer said. "This is insane. Search her if you have to but let the woman go."

"Fine," Duane said.

Several others fished their phones out and handed them over obediently. Enid produced her phone and handed it over. Duane stood expectantly in front of Billie and waited. Her mind raced. What could she say? "Oh, I think I left mine in the food truck," she said and glanced at Enid.

"Stop playing around and hand it over," Duane demanded.

"You left it in the taco truck," Marcel said. "I saw it on the side of the grill."

Duane turned around to face him. "I will search that truck and find you if the phone doesn't turn up," he said.

"Are you going to head down there and look

soon?" Marcel asked. "Because I left the window up and the door unlocked. I hope you do, so it doesn't disappear. That's my boss right there and I don't want to be responsible for someone swiping her phone."

Billie nodded her head. "You better hope my phone isn't gone, Marcel," she said as severely as she could make herself sound. "I have so many business contacts on that phone."

"Just get to your rooms and stay there," Duane said. He put his hand on Billie's shoulder to urge her forward.

"We are all up this way," Lucas said. He pointed toward the entrance.

"You're together?"

"Yeah, we're rooming together, and the women share a room, too," Marcel said quickly. Billie glanced at Enid. They both nodded their heads quickly. Billie ducked her head and walked slowly toward the curved walkway where her room was located. She pulled her key card out of her pocket. Marcel did the same.

They separated themselves slowly from the rest of the group and walked slowly toward their rooms. Billie swiped the card through her door and held it open for Enid.

"It's really pink in here," Enid whispered when the door closed behind her.

Billie nodded her head. "What happened a little while ago?" she asked.

Enid sat down in the small sitting area. "I was in my truck taking stock of how many cupcakes I had ready when about three of the police officers huddled together suddenly. That detective rushed into the room from somewhere in the dark and spoke to all of them," she said. "A few minutes later, they started rushing all of us out of the bays and around through these really narrow hallways. We ended up in the food court and the cops split us all up. That's about the time you found us."

"Okay, we are in some real trouble here," Billie said. She fished her phone out of her shirt and headed toward the bathroom. "Come here. You have to hear this." She waited for Enid to get to her feet and follow her. She closed the bathroom door behind them and turned on the fan.

"What are we doing in here?" Enid asked.

"Just listen," Billie said. She turned the voice recorder on and let it play. Enid's eyes grew round as she listened to the voices. When the shot rang out, she jumped in place and covered her mouth with her hand.

"Oh, my God!"

Billie nodded her head slowly. "We have to be really, really careful what we do at this point."

"He knows someone was out there," Enid said. "I think Collins is a bad cop."

"I don't think he is the only one," Billie said. "I'm not saying every one of them is, but after seeing that Duane fellow out there, I'm convinced that there are a few bad apples."

"I bet he killed Lincoln Mathers," Enid said. "We have to let the others know."

Billie nodded. "The first thing I'm going to do is take my phone charger out of the bedroom area and plug it in somewhere out of sight."

Enid was seated on the side of the bathtub. She stared hard at Billie. "Do you think they're going to search our rooms? Because if they find my room, they are going to know that I am not supposed to be here," she said. "My identification is still in my room."

Billie shrugged. "I don't think they will, and that officer Duane whatever would have to remember our faces and what was said," she explained. "I think we can figure our way out of that, but don't focus on it right now." She pressed her finger to her lips, opened the door, and headed directly to the bedroom for her phone charger. She motioned for Enid to join her when she passed the bathroom door again. She ventured toward the back of the area and searched for an electrical outlet.

"There," Enid whispered. She pointed to an outlet located behind an empty shelf. Billie rushed to the outlet and plugged her phone into it.

"I have to send the audio file to Sully," she said, referring to Detective Sullivan back home on Sea Glass Island.

"Do it," Enid said. "Right now. Don't hesitate. I don't want to be like those dummies in the horror movies that always talk forever about sending messages for help and wait until the monster is right outside of the window."

"Well, we're not waiting until the monster is right outside," Billie said. She sat down on the floor against the wall and picked up her phone, careful not to pull out the cord. She attached the audio file to an email addressed to Detective Sullivan, Chief Abernathy, and then to the Sea Glass Island Police Department's main email.

"Send a message to Sully, too," Enid urged. "You need to let her know that we're stuck here with these people."

"That's what I'm doing next," she said. She hit the send button and hoped that the emails reached their destinations. "Hold on while I call Sully."

"You shouldn't call her. Send her a text," Enid urged. "I don't want them to hear you talking or something."

Billie nodded and quickly typed out a message to Detective Sullivan. She included the location and a few details about what was going on. "They are confiscating cell phones," Billie wrote last. "Please come and bring the cavalry, but don't reply to this message. I'm scared what might happen if they find this phone and these messages."

Billie jumped when they heard someone pounding on the door. "Stall them," she whispered to Enid. She glanced at the last message she sent and deleted it along with the rest of them.

"Can I help you?" Enid asked whoever was at the door.

"We came to check for cell phones," a female voice said. Billie looked around the bathroom wall. Officer Burke stood in the main area of her room. "Are you here alone?"

Billie turned back to her cell phone. She quickly brought up the voice recorder app and deleted the audio file. "I'm back here," Billie called out. She pulled the cell phone charger out of the wall and stuffed both under the shelf. She stood up and rushed back out to the front.

"What were you doing back there?" Officer Burke asked her.

"Exploring," Billie said. "To be honest, I was looking for another way out of this room. With everything going on, it bothers me that there's just one exit."

"Yeah, it seems like that would be against fire code," Enid added.

"It usually is," Burke commented. She eyed the back suspiciously. "I'm here for your cell phone."

"Oh, did you guys find it?" Billie asked quickly. "We told the other officers that it was left in the taco truck."

"Which other officers?" Burke asked her.

"Well, they didn't tell us their names, exactly," Enid said. "But one officer called the other one 'Duane' or something."

"That's Officer Lundgren," Burke said. "What did he do?"

"About the cell phone or with the lady," Billie asked carefully. Enid gazed at her with big eyes.

"What lady?" Burke asked.

"Oh, there was a bit of an incident when a woman said she used to work as a paralegal and told him that it was illegal to take away our cell phones," Billie said.

"And what happened?" Burke asked. Billie did her best to read her face but wasn't able to tell what the police officer was thinking.

"Well, he acted like he was going to arrest her or something," Billie said. "She sort of started crying. I think she was just scared."

"What did this woman look like?" Burke asked.

"A little older than us," Enid said. "Long gray and blonde hair. Tall, a little pudgy."

"Okay," Burke said. "Do you know who the other officer was?"

Billie shook her head. "No, I didn't catch a name," she said.

"Burke, we have other places to be," another officer pushed the door open and said.

"Are we allowed out of our rooms?" Enid asked quickly. "I mean, the other officers said a few things, but I wasn't sure that I understood."

"Just stay in for now," Burke said. "I have to go."

Billie waited as Enid walked Officer Burke to the

door and closed it behind her. She turned back and closed her eyes in relief. "That was not fun," she said.

"We have to get to the guys," Billie said. "I really think we might be able to get to them from the back."

"I agree," Enid said. "We have to let them know what's going on."

"And we need to do it fast," Billie said.

CHAPTER 9

"I can't believe this is happening," Enid said. "First, they insist we make meals for everyone, then they refuse to let us leave this mall or use our own phones to call anyone. I just don't get it. How can they get away with this?"

Billie walked around the back of the room and looked in the dark space between the bathroom wall and the back of the store space. "There's something back here," Billie said. She stood between the wall and felt around. "I think there's a panel."

"What is it for?" Enid asked her.

"Hot water heater, maybe," Billie said. She felt along the top of the panel. "There are screws. We have to find something to use as a screwdriver."

"On it," Enid said. She disappeared into the front

of the room and returned with a knife from the kitchenette.

"Perfect," Billie said. She took the knife from her and returned to the panel. She squinted to see while she inserted the sharp end of the knife into the first of six screws. She collected the screws and shoved them in her pocket, then worked the panel loose. "I'm right. The hot water heater is back here. But there is some space around it and room behind it. I think the units share the hot water heater."

"And that means we should be able to get to the guys through here." Enid grinned. Billie nodded and crawled carefully inside. She couldn't see very far, but from what she could see, cobwebs were everywhere. She swatted at the area with her hands before she climbed past the hot water heater.

"Can you go back and get my phone out from under the shelf? Just leave the cord there and push the shelf back over it."

"I'll be right back," Enid said and left her again.

"There's only about two feet of space around the heater," she called back to Enid. She hoped no spiders were crawling down her back when she flattened herself against the wall. As soon as she made it past the hot water heater, she brushed off her arms and every area she could reach with her hands. Enid made it past and joined her in the small space behind it. Billie felt around on the wall and located the panel to the other room.

"What are we going to do now?" Enid asked her.

"Push on it and hope the panel gives way easily," Billie said. She felt for the edges and began pushing hard on the corners. She ignored the part of her brain that cringed each time she felt something wispy against her skin. Spiders were not her favorite thing to think about when she was deep in their realm.

"Any luck?" Enid whispered behind her.

"I think if I give it a good push with both hands, it might give," Billie said. She pushed the top right corner with both hands. The panel gave slightly. She could hear the metallic plink of the small screw hit the floor. She moved her hands to the top left corner and quietly cheered when another screw popped out and hit the floor. Two more screws popped out and Billie was able to push the panel through.

"I hope this is their room," Enid said when she followed Billie through the panel.

"Let's go quietly until we know," Billie whispered. She went slowly through the back portion of the old store and motioned for Enid to stay behind her. She could see light ahead of her. "Marcel? Marcel, it's Billie."

They could hear someone shuffling around in the next room. Billie tensed up until she spotted Marcel in the shadows. "What on earth? How did you get in here?" Marcel asked. Lucas showed up right behind him.

"Billie figured out that our rooms share a hot water heater," Enid said. "We found a way around it and pushed the panel in."

"We have to talk to you," Billie said. "And we need to keep this quick and quiet."

"Yeah, the cops were just at our door asking us for cell phones," Enid said.

"I don't see how they can do that," Lucas said. "That doesn't seem right or legal at all for them to hold us here and cut off communication from the outside world."

Billie pulled her phone out of her pocket. "There's something you guys need to hear."

"Wait, I thought you deleted the files and the text messages to Sully," Enid asked.

"Who is Sully?" Lucas asked.

"Detective Sullivan," Marcel explained. "From the island. Good friend of ours."

"Okay," Lucas said. "You texted this detective?"

"And sent her this," Billie said. She located the email she had sent in her email app and tapped the audio file. "Maybe I should have thought a little more thoroughly about this and erased the sent files as well, but I'm glad you guys can hear it for yourselves." Billie hit play and waited while the men listened to the conversation. All four of them jumped when the shot rang out. Even Billie, who knew it was coming, found herself startled by it all again.

"I think you should remove any trace of that from your phone," Lucas said. "Right away. Don't take any chances with this police department."

"I can't believe what we just heard," Marcel said. "It seems Detective Collins is a killer."

"I bet he's responsible for Debra Millstead's death as well," Enid said.

Lucas nodded. "That's why I'm telling you to get rid of that file," he said. "If there is any chance that phone is found on you, we could all be in trouble."

"They can't hold us here forever," Marcel said. "I mean, surely someone somewhere is going to start asking questions."

Billie nodded her head. "That's what we're all hoping for," she said. "But the truth of the matter is that at least part of the local police department here in this town is corrupt. It won't be forever, but I surely don't want to spend another night here."

"He's right, Billie," Enid said. She glanced

nervously at the phone. "Erase the emails in the sent folder, too. No need to take any chances."

"Maybe Sully got the emails, and she will come and end all of this," Marcel said.

Lucas nodded and looked directly at Billie. "Maybe so, but in the meantime, the four of us have to keep our wits about us," he said. "We can't be seen with a phone, and we need to be careful what we say if and when we are around others."

Billie nodded. "For the time being, I think we need to stay put. I don't think all of the cops are bad, but it might be hard to tell the good from the not so good."

"It's also possible that the good don't recognize the bad," Enid said.

"Why can't we play that audio in front of every-one?" Marcel asked. "Surely there are more of us than there are of them. We can overpower the bad ones."

"Only the bad guys have the guns, man," Lucas said. "I had the same thought while we were listening to the audio, but it is just too dangerous for us to take any chances."

Billie nodded. "When I was down there in the warehouse area I had the same thought," she said. "I wanted to come out shouting about what I had just seen and heard, but Collins knows there was someone down there."

"That's why he's pushing so hard to separate us from our phones," Lucas said. "I bet he knows he has limited time before he has to let everyone go. He's just hoping he gets to whoever overheard him downstairs before that happens."

CHAPTER 10

Billie and Enid scrambled back to the water heater closet when a loud knock came on the door of Marcel's room. Enid slipped in behind the water heater first. Billie followed and pulled the panel back in front of them and held it in place. She could hear voices from the front of the room and hoped the cops at the door were the good kind and not the corrupt under Detective Collin's influence.

"What if they come back to our door?" Enid asked. "I swear I just heard another knock coming from the other side."

"Do you think they might?" Billie asked. She hadn't considered the possibility. "Can you go back out there and turn on the bathroom light and fan? Shut the door and tell them that I am in the shower or something."

"On it," Enid said. "Hang tight."

Billie nodded in the darkness. She set the panel to Marcel's room back on the floor and helped Enid pull the panel from her room back into place. She waited in silence and prayed that the conversations occurring on either side of the water heater were over quickly. The water heater kicked on behind her. Enid must have turned the shower on in the bathroom to convince their visitors that Billie really was in the shower.

A second later, Enid called out from the living room space. "Hey, Billie," Enid shouted. "If you can hurry up in there, we're supposed to gather down in the food court again."

Billie moved carefully around the hot water heater and slipped back through the panel. She walked slowly around the back of the bathroom and looked carefully to see whether or not it was clear. She padded silently across the floor until she was in reach of the bathroom door. She reached her hand out and slowly twisted the bathroom door open, then eased it shut behind her.

As fast as she could, Billie slipped off her socks and shoes and splashed water on her hair and face.

She wrapped her hair up in a towel and shut the water off. She opened the door and called out to Enid. "Did you say something?" she asked.

"Yeah, I did," Enid's face appeared in her view. "I said the police have asked us all to gather downstairs in the food court again."

"Right now?" Billie asked. She took the towel out of her hair and pretended to dry it.

"Yes, right now," Officer Duane Lundgren appeared behind Enid and answered for her. "Get yourself together and get down there in less than five minutes."

"Okay, can I finish getting dressed first?" Billie asked.

"Five minutes!" Officer Lundgren turned around on his heels and left again. Billie sighed in relief and turned back to the bathroom. She slipped back into her shoes and socks and pulled her hair back in a ponytail. She looked around the bathroom and sprayed herself with some of the body spray she found on the shelf and headed back out to join Enid.

"What's going on?" she whispered when they headed out of the room.

"I don't know," Enid said. "He just said everyone is supposed to gather down there."

"Okay," Billie said. "Maybe they're going to let

us go." They walked around the curved walkway toward the escalator.

"What did you do with your phone?" Enid asked her when they were halfway down.

"Oh, no," Billie said. She clenched her fist to prevent herself from reaching back to touch the phone in her back pocket. "It's still in my pocket."

"Did you erase everything on it?"

Billie slowly nodded her head. "I think so," she said as they got off the escalator. "At least, I hope I did."

They fell silent as they walked down into the seating area. Billie quickly scanned the crowd for Marcel and Lucas. She spotted them on the far side of the room and signaled to Enid to follow her.

"Sit down," Detective Collins barked to the room at large. Billie continued walking. "Right now. Stop moving around and sit down right where you are."

Billie stopped moving and looked up. They were halfway across the room. Detective Collins pointed directly at her when he barked his last order. Enid grabbed her by the arm and led her to the table directly in front of them. "We don't need any extra attention," Enid whispered. Billie nodded and shot a look in Marcel's direction. He locked eyes with her and nodded slightly in return. At least they knew where each was located.

"What are we doing down here now?" a man called out from the back of the room.

"Just sit down and shut up until you're told to speak." Officer Duane Lundgren scowled at the man.

"How long are you going to keep us here?" another voice called out.

"Forever if you all don't shut your mouths," Officer Lundgren said.

"That's enough," Detective Collins said. Billie was unsure who he was speaking to, but the room fell silent. "We have been patient with all of you to this point, but it's clear that someone has been sneaking around this mall in unauthorized areas. I will be merciful to the person who steps forward and admits it."

"What in Hades is going on here? I'm getting sick of this clown show. We all came here to attend a business conference. You people are walking around here like we're prisoners! This isn't how investigations are done." The speaker was a middle-aged man dressed in a white dress shirt and a tie.

"Yeah," another man stood up in the middle of the room. Before Billie could think, Officer Duane Lungren approached the man in the tie and leaned so close to him that the man nearly fell over. When he landed back on his chair, a collective gasp filled the room.

"What on earth?" Several women began whispering to each other.

"Anybody else?" Detective Collins jerked his head at Duane, directing the officer back behind him. "That's what I thought. Now, back to what I was saying before. Someone here has been sneaking around the mall where they are not supposed to be. We aren't leaving here until whoever it is steps forward and takes responsibility for their actions."

The room fell silent. Billie exchanged looks with Lucas and Marcel. She knew exactly who the detective was looking for, and she was terrified of what might happen if they found out it was her. She was equally scared of what would happen to the others if she didn't come forward.

Lucas caught her eye again and slowly shook his head. Billie looked at Enid and debated what to do next. If she stood up, she could maybe end the nightmare for everyone else. After all, this small, suburban police department couldn't hold this large group of people indefinitely. Others would come looking for them.

A movement caught her eye. She looked up and

gasped. Lincoln Mathers had entered the room. He stood next to Detective Collins with a smirk on his face. Billie felt the muscles in her arms and legs weaken, and then go limp.

"Well, I guess we have a winner," Detective Collins said. It was the last thing she heard before the room went dark around her.

CHAPTER 11

Billie woke to yelling all around her. It took her several moments for her memory to catch up with her. She was not in the commissary kitchen building or anywhere near the festival grounds on Sea Glass Island. She was nowhere close to her island home at all. She was miles and miles away in a shopping mall that had been turned into a convention venue.

But the convention had not taken place. Instead, a woman had been murdered right in front of her eyes, and the eyes of another hundred or more souls who were in attendance. Since then, the police department had sequestered them in the stores converted into motel rooms. Their phones had been confiscated from them, essentially cutting them off from the outside world. Questions about what was going on and when they could leave were left with no answers.

Then there was the second murder. Billie had hidden silently in the dark and listened to what she thought was the murder of Lincoln Mathers. Only now, here he stood. Billie blinked a half-dozen times to focus her eyes on the man standing in front of her.

"I think the rest of you need to return to your rooms," Detective Collins said. "Now. That wasn't a suggestion."

"Maybe we don't want to go anywhere," Lucas shouted. Billie turned to look at him and shook her head this time. She turned back to the detective. He glared at her with a terrifying gleam in his eyes. Billie swallowed hard.

"I don't care what you want," Collins shouted back. "And for anyone else who wants to complain, you should know that we've had another murder. A man's body was found in the warehouse section of the mall. That is why I ordered all of you back to your rooms. I don't know who committed this crime, but I have an inkling about it."

"Who died? Who was it?" Billie asked. She found her voice at last.

"As if you don't know," Detective Collins snapped at her.

"I don't know, Detective," Billie said. "How could I know?"

"Calvin Greer was found dead in the inventory storage section of the receiving bay," Officer Burke stepped forward and answered. "He was shot in the abdomen and left for dead."

"And you Miss Halifax are the number one subject in his murder," Detective Collins said.

"Oh, am I? Can you tell me why I would be a suspect?"

"Because I saw your reaction, Miss Halifax," Detective Collins hissed at her.

"What was that?" Lucas called out. "Can you say that louder for the rest of us?"

"He said it because he saw my reaction to seeing Lincoln Mather's still alive."

"I think you better shut your mouth while you're ahead," Detective Collins whispered harshly.

Billie looked around the room again. She was safer in front of a hundred different people than she ever would be in a room alone with the detective, she decided. "You're right. I was in the dark part of the mall past the receiving bay. I was there and overheard quite the conversation. And I did receive a shock when I saw Lincoln here still alive," she said.

"That's enough," Detective Collins shouted. He

flicked his hand toward Officer Burke and Officer Rogers. "You two. Grab her and shut her up! Now! Move!"

"Wait," Billie said, backing up. "Before you do, you should know that it was Detective Collins down there in the dark when the gun went off. He was with Lincoln Mathers. They fought and the gun went off. I don't know how Calvin Greer is involved, but it wasn't me. I didn't have anything to do with this."

"Burke! Rogers! Shut her up," Detective Collins screamed.

"Why didn't you say anything before about what happened?" Officer Rogers questioned her. Neither he nor his partner made any moves toward her.

"Because I don't know who I can trust," Billie said. "I have seen unlawful officers do and say terrible things. I've seen my own food truck managers extorted out of their time and inventory to feed all of you. Nothing about this place or this police department is trustworthy."

"I've heard enough," Detective Collins said. "If no one else is going to shut this woman up, I will."

"Before you do that, Detective Collins, you should know that a recording was made of your conversation with Lincoln Mathers," Lucas stood up and spoke so loudly that his voice echoed across the vast space. "And a copy of the audio file was sent out to other members of law enforcement."

"What is he talking about?" Detective Collins asked. He pulled his gun out of his vest holster and waved it around. "What are you talking about?" He turned directly toward Lucas and aimed his weapon.

"Whoa, whoa," Officer Rogers said. He pulled out his own weapon and aimed it at Collins. Duane did the same thing and pointed it at Rogers. Officer Burke pulled her weapon and aimed it at Collins and then at Lucas.

"Everyone needs to just simmer down right now," Officer Burke said. She turned to Detective Collins. "What is going on here? Why haven't you called in more help or the state police? Why are we still holding these people hostage here?"

Detective Collins shifted his focus. He turned around and trained his weapon on Billie. "You killed Debra Millstead and then you killed Calvin Greer. I ought to kill you right here on the spot."

"Don't do it, Detective," Lucas said. Billie looked to her right. Her food truck manager had pulled a weapon of his own and aimed it straight at the rogue detective. He held the gun with his right hand and reached into his back pocket with his left. He pulled something shiny and metal and waved it in the air. "Special Agent Lucas Malloy, FBI. You, sir, have the right to remain silent."

CHAPTER 12

"FBI?" Marcel asked him a moment later. Officer Rogers reached the detective first and relieved him of his firearm. Officer Burke tackled Duane Lundgren to the ground before he could fire off his own weapon. Billie stood in the middle of it all in utter shock. After several moments, it dawned on her what Lucas had just said.

"So, you're not from the culinary school?"

Lucas secured Detective Collins from Officer Rogers and laughed. "I am alumni, actually," he said. "But that was before I decided to try my hand at running after bad guys instead of running a kitchen," he said. He raised his head up and looked at the upper level. "Okay, you can come out now."

Billie looked up in time to see a dozen men and

women all dressed in street clothes with guns drawn step out of the shadows. She raised her hand when she recognized a familiar redheaded detective. "Sully."

Detective Sullivan holstered her own firearm and headed down the steps. "You didn't tell me you were hiring field agents as bratwurst truck managers, Billie."

"That's because I had no idea," Billie said. She turned to Lucas. "Obviously your name is not Lucas Hibberd, Agent Malloy. What is going on here?"

"For that, you're going to need to have a long conversation with a certain attorney," Lucas said. He handed Collins off to another officer and turned back to Billie. "Alex Regent knew all about this. He has another manager waiting in the wings to take my place."

"Then, what was this all about?" Billie asked, still stunned. She turned to Sully. "Did you know?"

Sully shook her head. "Not until two days ago," she said. "We were on standby in case things went sour."

"And a good thing you were," Lucas said. "Billie, when you were able to obtain that audio recording, you put an end to a case that we never thought would get solved so quickly. We only wanted to be in the area to see how the officers handled themselves. We never expected all of this to occur."

Billie shook her head. "You both are saying a lot of words really fast, and I feel like I have missed half of the information. What case? How did Alex get involved? And why didn't anyone tell me about it?"

"Let's just sum it up like this," Lucas said. "We have been watching the police department in this town for a couple of years now. We had multiple complaints about a number of things, but no way to actually prove anything. When this conference came to our attention, we saw the perfect in."

"That's when the FBI contacted your attorney and worked out a deal to put an agent on site for the conference," Sully explained. "They wanted to be close to the police department and knew there would be officers here at the event. We didn't know everything was going to escalate as far as it did, which was unfortunate, but now everything has come to a head, and I suppose that's what we wanted in the bigger picture."

"We had an informant that filled us in on some rather unsavory activities happening here in the old mall," Lucas said. "Lincoln Mathers was my informant, and he helped us get closer to the evidence we needed to find the center of an extortion ring, a

2

money laundering scam, and a horde of other criminal activity stemming from this place."

"Why did Collins pretend to kill Lincoln Mathers, then?" Billie asked, suddenly aware of another ten people being led away in handcuffs, including Duane Lundgren and the server behind the breakfast counter that same morning.

"Collins knew someone was down there," Lucas said. "He knew if he pretended it was Lincoln who was killed and then brought him back to life later, he'd get a reaction from whoever was down there."

"That and probably for the same reason he had Debra poisoned," Sully said.

Lucas nodded. "Lincoln, Debra, and Collins were all involved. This old mall offers the perfect setting for loose bookkeeping practices. Debra Millstead is the one who came up with the plan and she started wanting to take control and Collins didn't like that."

"But when Collins got involved, he started blackmailing his cohorts for more money. He had the power to make things go south for anyone at any time, given his job," Sully said.

"But why did Calvin Greer have to die?" Billie asked. "What did he do?"

"That was a case of wrong place, wrong time," Lucas said. "When you were down in the basement with Collins and Mathers, you weren't the only one. Calvin had overheard a previous conversation between Debra Millstead and Detective Collins. He went to Lincoln with his concerns and the entire conversation was a setup, but Lincoln didn't know about the murder part. He never expected Collins to actually have gotten to Calvin first."

"Everything came apart when you just happened to be there," Sully said. "Like Lucas said, that recording you sent shortened a very tedious and dangerous investigation by months."

"When you were able to sneak into our room and share that with us, that was all the evidence I needed to move forward," Lucas said. "Detective Sullivan here was already on standby."

"What happens now?" Marcel asked.

"For one thing, the entire police department will come under the control of the local sheriff's department while there is an investigation into the charges with the department," Lucas said.

"And you guys are free to head back to the island and stay off of the mainland for a while," Sully said with a grin. "Chief Abernathy and I will get statements from each of you."

"Okay, but who's going to run the bratwurst

truck?" Enid asked. "After the past few days, I thought we were sort of a team, the four of us."

"We can still be a team," Lucas said. He draped one arm around Marcel's shoulders. "Since you helped wrap this investigation up for us so fast, I thought I might stick around for a couple of weeks and help you run the truck while you wait for the real manager to arrive," Lucas said to Billie.

"You're going to run a food truck and be an FBI agent at the same time?" she asked flatly.

"No, I have more than a month of paid time off coming to me," Lucas said. "What better way to spend it than by walking the beach every morning and serving my famous pear and bacon brats every night?"

"An agent and a comedian," Sully said, rolling her eyes.

"Exactly how much longer do we have to put up with this guy?" Marcel asked. "Will the real bratwurst chef please step forward."

"Hey, watch it, Johnson," Lucas said. "I might be in law enforcement, but I am a force to be reckoned with in the kitchen."

"I told you," Sully said to Billie. "He's an agent and a comedian."

"Hey, you can't say much, Sully," Billie reminded

her. "I remember a very eager detective who worked at my cupcake truck a few times…"

***

If you enjoyed Wurst Day Ever and are looking for more food truck adventures, check out A Real Jam, today!

AUTHOR'S NOTE

I'd love to hear your thoughts on my books, the storylines, and anything else that you'd like to comment on—reader feedback is very important to me. My contact information, along with some other helpful links, is listed on the next page. If you'd like to be on my list of "folks to contact" with updates, release and sales notifications, etc.… just shoot me an email and let me know. Thanks for reading!

Also…

… if you're looking for more great reads, Summer Prescott Books publishes several popular series by outstanding Cozy Mystery authors.

CONTACT GRETCHEN ALLEN

Visit my website for more information about new releases, upcoming projects, and be sure to check out my special Members Only section for extra freebies and fun!

Website: www.gretchenallen.com

Email: contact@gretchenallen.com

Visit the Summer Prescott Books website to find even more great reads!

Made in the USA
Coppell, TX
12 May 2023

16738916R00069